Elisa
the Adventure Fairy

Special thanks to
Rachel Elliot

ORCHARD BOOKS
338 Euston Road, London NW1 3BH
Orchard Books Australia
Level 17/207 Kent Street, Sydney, NSW 2000
A Paperback Original

First published in 2011 by Orchard Books

HiT entertainment

Illustrations © Orchard Books 2011

A CIP catalogue record for this book is available
from the British Library.

ISBN 978 1 40830 296 4

3 5 7 9 10 8 6 4

Printed in Great Britain

The paper and board used in this paperback are natural recyclable
products made from wood grown in sustainable forests. The
manufacturing processes conform to the environmental regulations
of the country of origin.

Orchard Books is a division of Hachette Children's Books,
an Hachette UK company

www.hachette.co.uk

Elisa
the Adventure
Fairy

by Daisy Meadows

ORCHARD

www.rainbowmagic.co.uk

The Fairyland Palace

The Orangery

The Lake

Maze

Petting Zoo

PETTING

Topiary Garden

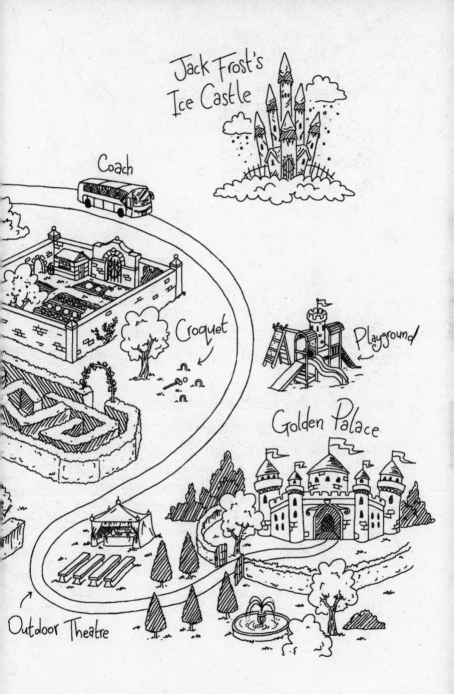

The fairies are planning a magical ball,
With guests of honour and fun for them all.
They're expecting a night full of laughter and cheer
But they'll get a shock when my goblins appear!

Adventures and treats will be things of the past,
And I'll beat those troublesome fairies at last.
My iciest magic will blast through the room
And the world will be plunged into grimness
and gloom!

Contents

A Ghostly Surprise   9

Behind the Bookcase   19

Jewel Trackers   31

Rachel at Risk!   41

Tricksy Fairies   53

The Spirit of Adventure   65

A Ghostly Surprise

"I wonder what adventures Louis and Caroline have arranged for us this evening," said Kirsty Tate, smiling at her best friend, Rachel Walker, across the grand banqueting table.

It was the spring holidays, and they were staying at Golden Palace for Kids' Week, a special event for children. Louis and Caroline were the palace stewards, and they had been looking after the children all week as if they were royalty.

"I'm sure they'll have something wonderful planned," said Rachel, scraping the last bit of strawberry ice cream from her silver bowl. The grand Banqueting Hall was looking very beautiful, full of twinkling candles and lights. Kirsty gazed thoughtfully out of the large, round window at the end of the hall. It was twilight, but she could see the silhouette of the palace's crumbling old tower.

It rose up majestically from the
battlements against the purple sky, and it
was the only place that the children were
not allowed to go.

"I wish they would let us climb all the
way up to the top of the tower," Kirsty
said. "I'd love to explore it!"

"It sounds a bit scary to me," said
a girl called Victoria, who was sitting
next to Kirsty. "I'm not feeling very
adventurous."

Rachel and Kirsty exchanged a secret smile. They had already had plenty of adventures that week, helping their friends, the Princess Fairies, get their magic tiaras back from Jack Frost and his goblins. So far they had found the tiaras that belonged to Princess Honor the Happy Days Fairy, Princess Demi the Dressing-Up Fairy and Princess Anya the Cuddly Creatures Fairy. But there were still four more to find.

Each of the Princess Fairies looked after a special area of fairy magic. Without their magical tiaras, things would go wrong in both the human and fairy worlds. Jack Frost and his mischievous goblins had stolen them during a ball at the Fairyland Palace, and brought them to the human world.

Queen Titania had not been able to stop him from taking the tiaras, but she had used her magic to make sure that they would be hidden at Golden Palace. Now the fairies were depending on Rachel and Kirsty to help them find the tiaras.

Just then, Victoria gave a cry of surprise. "Look!" she exclaimed. "Why didn't we notice that before?"

There was a tall vase in the centre of the big banqueting table, containing long-stemmed pink roses. But Victoria had noticed that there was something tucked among the roses – a mysterious scroll of parchment. She picked it up and read it aloud:

To our Kids' Week guests

"Ooh, it must be about tonight's activity!" said Rachel excitedly. "Quick, open it!"

Victoria took the scroll from among the roses, being careful not to damage any of the petals. She unrolled it and everyone gathered around her to see what it said. The instructions were written in large, gold letters.

Meet us where adventures flow
Among the pages white as snow.
A room containing tales of glory
Within each bound and printed story.

"That sounds a bit complicated," said a boy called Arthur.

"I hope it isn't anything too difficult," said Victoria.

Rachel and Kirsty exchanged a surprised glance. The other children had seemed to enjoy their other activities and adventures. But now they weren't even interested in solving the riddle.

"Pages and printed stories," said Rachel. "What room contains those things? Oh, I know! The library!"

"You're right!" said Kirsty. "Come on, I expect they'll be waiting for us there."

The children left the Banqueting Hall and walked across the polished entrance hall to the foot of the Grand Staircase. Flickering candles lit their way as they walked slowly up towards the library. Suddenly, Victoria and Arthur stopped in their tracks. Arthur turned white, and Victoria raised a trembling hand to point to a shadow on the wall.

"It's a g…ghost!" she squeaked.

Everyone except Kirsty and Rachel shrieked and clutched at each other. The girls caught a fleeting glimpse of a dark shape, but then it vanished.

"Did you see that?" asked Kirsty.

Rachel nodded. "I couldn't tell what it was, though," she said. "It disappeared too quickly."

"It was a ghost," said Arthur in a terrified whisper. "A ghost of a king from long ago who used to live here."

"I'm sure it can't really have been a ghost," said Rachel sensibly.

"It was probably just a weird shadow from the candle flames," Kirsty added.

They both felt a bit surprised that the other children were so scared!

"Let's run the rest of the way!" said Victoria in a shaky voice.

Behind the Bookcase

They all hurried up the stairs and darted into the library. It was lined with bookcases made of polished oak, and the lamps around the room were burning brightly. On a rug in the middle of the room, a large cloth covered a mysterious pile. But the palace stewards were nowhere to be seen.

"Where are Louis and Caroline?" asked Kirsty, looking around.

"M…aybe the ghost has taken them to the tower," stammered Arthur. "M…maybe they know that it's haunted, and that's why we're not allowed up there!"

A squeaking sound made them jump, and then one of the bookcases began to move. It spun around and everyone shrieked…then burst into laughter. Caroline and Louis were revealed in front of them!

"Sorry to scare you all," chuckled Louis. "We thought you might like to see one of our secret hiding places!"

"How does it work?" asked Rachel in excitement.

Louis showed them a vase on one of the shelves.

"This isn't really a vase at all," he explained. "It's a secret lever!"

He tipped the vase towards him by its neck, and the bookcase spun around again, taking Louis with it and hiding him from sight.

They heard him chuckle on the other side of the bookcase, and then it turned and brought him back into the library.

"It's a wonderful trick," said Kirsty. "I wish we had one of those at home!"

"I hope we didn't frighten you," said Caroline.

"It's just that we had a bit of a scare on the Grand Staircase," Victoria explained.

 When the stewards heard what the children had seen, Caroline shook her head with a smile.

"I promise you, there's no such thing as ghosts," she said. "What you saw was probably the shadows of clouds scudding across the moon."

"We thought that the ghost might have taken you to the tower," Arthur whispered. "We guessed it was haunted."

"The tower isn't haunted," Caroline assured him. "But it's very old and some of the steps are missing, so that's why we ask you not to go up there."

"Now," said Louis in a cheerful voice. "Get into pairs, everyone."

Rachel clasped Kirsty's hand. They watched as Louis and Caroline pulled away the cloth on the rug. Underneath was a pile of party bags.

"Help yourselves. One bag per pair," said Caroline.

Rachel and Kirsty excitedly chose a bag and peeped inside. It contained two torches, a small scroll and two crowns.

"All the crowns are missing their jewels," Louis explained. "Tonight's activity is a treasure hunt around the palace to find the jewels!"

The children gave little gasps of excitement, and Louis grinned at them.

"On the scrolls you will find some clues," he said. "By following the clues, you will find the missing jewel stickers to complete your crowns. The clues for each pair are different, so you will be spread throughout the palace.

The winner is the first team to collect
all their jewels and return to the library.
Good luck!"

The children moved out into the
corridor. Rachel and Kirsty felt very
excited, but the others
looked a bit glum.

"I'm not very
good at solving
clues," they
heard one boy
mutter.

"I just feel
like reading a
book instead,"
Victoria said.

"Well, I
can't wait to get
started!" said Rachel.

She pulled out the
scroll and read
the first clue to
Kirsty. "Look
for something
that protects
a knight in
battle, then
search behind
the lion."

"Something
that protects
a knight in
battle," Kirsty
repeated. "It must
be some sort of armour."

"Remember the armoury we visited on
the first day?" Rachel said eagerly. "Let's
start our search there."

Rachel and Kirsty hurried to the armoury. Inside, suits of armour stood to attention in a row, and the walls were hung with heavy tapestries of ancient battles. In the centre of the room was a display of antique shields, all painted with brightly coloured pictures.

"Kirsty, I think our clue is telling us to look behind a shield!" said Rachel. "A shield protects a knight in battle. I

bet that one of these shields has a lion painted on it!"

The girls rushed forward to examine the shields one by one, looking carefully at all the pictures.

"A unicorn…a bear…an eagle…" said Kirsty, moving along one side of the display.

"A wolf…a panther…a LION!" exclaimed Rachel. "Here it is!"

Jewel Trackers

Together, Kirsty and Rachel looked behind the shield for a jewel sticker.

"There's nothing there," said Kirsty in disappointment. "We must have got the clue wrong."

Rachel looked all around the armoury.

"There's nothing else here with a lion on it," she said. "I don't understand."

"Come on," said Kirsty. "Let's go back to the library and ask Louis and Caroline if we've made a mistake."

They walked out of the armoury and bumped into Arthur and Victoria, who were looking very fed up.

"Hello," said Rachel. "Have you found your first jewel yet?"

"No," Arthur said crossly. "These clues are silly."

"We solved the clue, but we couldn't find the jewel sticker," said Victoria.

"Same here," Kirsty told her.

"I'm not sure I want to carry on with the treasure hunt

if it's going to be this hard," said Victoria with a sigh.

"Don't give up yet," said Rachel.

"I'm sure we just have to think about the clues again. After all, treasure hunts aren't supposed to be too easy."

"OK," said Arthur, looking a little bit more cheerful. "Come on, Victoria, I've got another idea."

He hurried away down the corridor, and Rachel and Kirsty looked at each other.

"It's strange that everyone seems so ready to give up, isn't it?" said Kirsty thoughtfully.

"Everyone except us!" Rachel replied with a grin. "Come on, where shall we look next?"

They set off down the corridor in the opposite direction. Night had fallen, and small lamps jutted out of the thick stone wall, giving off a warm orange glow. There was a narrow lancet window cut into the wall ahead of them, and the light there was flickering.

"Is one of the lamps going out?" Rachel wondered.

The girls hurried over to the window and had a wonderful surprise. Princess Elisa the Adventure Fairy was hovering in the opening! She looked even more beautiful than they remembered in her silky harem pants and sparkly vest top.

"Hello Rachel, hello Kirsty!" she said in a tinkling voice. "It's wonderful to see you again."

"It's good to see you too, Princess Elisa," said Kirsty eagerly. "We're in the middle of a treasure hunt,

but I think something has gone wrong.

We were supposed to find jewel stickers
for our crowns, but they're not where the
clues say they should be."

Elisa nodded sadly. "I know," she said.
"The treasure hunt has gone wrong
because my tiara is still missing. That's
why I've come here this evening – we
must find the tiara, or it won't just be the
treasure hunt that goes wrong."

"What do you mean?" Rachel gasped.
"My tiara helps me to protect

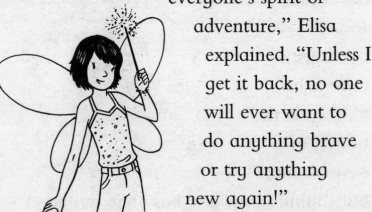

everyone's spirit of
adventure," Elisa
explained. "Unless I
get it back, no one
will ever want to
do anything brave
or try anything
new again!"

"That explains why the other boys and girls aren't very excited about the treasure hunt," said Kirsty.

"And they were all really scared by the shadow on the Grand Staircase," agreed Rachel. "But Elisa, why aren't we affected? Kirsty and I feel just as adventurous as ever!"

Elisa pointed to the lockets that hung around the girls' necks.

"Your lockets contain magical fairy dust," she said. "That has protected your spirit of adventure. Plus you have already helped three of the other Princesses, so their magic protects you, too!"

Just then, something sparkling on the floor caught Rachel's eye.

"Look, a jewel sticker!" she cried, stooping to pick it up. "It's a ruby. This must be one of the missing stickers for the crowns!"

"Something else is sparkling over there," said Kirsty, hurrying forwards. "Yes, it's another jewel sticker! An emerald."

Suddenly, the lamps flickered and went out. The only light came from the moon that shone through the narrow lancet window.

"Rachel, weren't there some torches in the party bag?" asked Kirsty.

Rachel pulled out the torches and handed one to Kirsty. They switched them on, and the yellow beams picked out another sticker sparkling further along the corridor floor.

"It's a trail," said Elisa eagerly. "Let's follow it!"

Rachel at Risk!

The girls walked forward slowly, with
Elisa fluttering between them. Their
torches picked out another sticker,
and another, and another. Sparkling
diamonds, amethysts and sapphires led
them down a long passageway, through
a tiny door and out onto the battlements
that ran along the front of the palace.

Stars glimmered in the indigo sky as they followed the stickers to the foot of a narrow, winding staircase. Rachel and Kirsty looked up and saw that they were standing beneath the crumbling tower.

"Why have you stopped?" asked Elisa.

"We're not allowed to go up there," Kirsty explained. "The steps aren't safe to climb."

The girls felt very disappointed, but Elisa smiled.

"You can fly up instead," she said. "Then you won't have to touch the steps at all!"

Elisa waved her
wand, and a shower
of silvery fairy
dust sprinkled
over the girls.
Shimmering
wings appeared
on their backs
and they shrank
to fairy size,
together with their
torches and party bag.

"Thank you!" said Rachel, fluttering
into the air and twirling around in
delight. "Now we can explore the tower
without breaking the rules!"

Eagerly, the girls and Elisa zoomed up
the winding staircase. Then, suddenly,
a strange shadow loomed over them!

"Quick, hide!" cried Elisa. They ducked into an arrow-slit cut into the wall, holding their breaths. The ghost came closer and closer...and then a green foot appeared on the stairs above them. It wasn't a ghost – it was a goblin trudging down the stairs!

"*More* jewel stickers," he was grumbling under his breath. "I've spent all day looking for jewel stickers, and now Jack Frost wants even *more*! He gets to play the king of Golden Palace and boss us around all the time. It's not fair!"

"So the tower isn't haunted," whispered Rachel as the goblin stomped crossly past, muttering. "Jack Frost and his goblins are hiding up there!"

"Do you think your tiara could be there too, Elisa?" asked Kirsty, hopefully.

"We have to find out!" said Elisa in a determined voice. "Come on!"

They darted out of their hiding place and zoomed up until they reached a heavy wooden door. On the other side, someone was making a lot of noise.

"I recognise that voice!" Elisa
whispered to the girls.

"So do I," said Rachel, sounding
concerned. "It's Jack Frost!"

Kirsty noticed another arrow-slit
further along the wall.

"Let's fly outside the tower and try to
find a way into the room,"
she suggested.

They
fluttered out
through the
arrow-slit
and saw
that one of
the walls had

almost completely crumbled away. They
flicked their tiny torches off and peered
over the rubble.

The room was faintly lit by three candles in a candelabra, and Jack Frost was sitting on a moth-eaten throne in the centre. He had one leg crooked over the arm of the throne, and a beautiful tiara sat on top of his spiky head. It was much too small for him. As the girls watched, it slipped sideways and he shoved it back in place.

"Fetch me more jewels!" he was bellowing at the goblins in the room. "Bring me more cake! Sing me a song! Paint my portrait!"

The goblins were scurrying around in
a panic. One was carrying a lopsided
cake with grey icing, but he tripped. The
cake flew through the air and landed at
Jack Frost's feet with a loud squelch.

"Idiot!" roared Jack Frost, bouncing
up and down in his seat. The tiara slid
sideways again and dangled from his
ear. "Bring me cake *now*!"

A goblin in a black beret was standing
beside an easel, angrily waving a fistful
of paintbrushes at a third goblin, who
was stamping on his tubes of paint,
sending coloured blobs squirting through
the air.

In the corner, a very small goblin was
strumming an out-of-tune guitar and
squawking loudly.

"I think he's *singing*," said Rachel,

covering her ears with her hands. "I wish he'd stop!"

"No," said Kirsty, her eyes sparkling. "I've got an idea. It's quite dark in there, and it's total chaos. Maybe with everything that's going on, Jack Frost won't notice us grabbing the tiara!"

"It's worth a try," said Elisa, always ready for adventure.

Moving cautiously, they flew through the hole in the wall towards Jack Frost, keeping to the shadows. They got closer and closer, and Rachel's heart was hammering. Soon they would be near enough to touch the tiara!

Suddenly, Jack Frost jerked his head to bark an order to a goblin, and Rachel jumped. Her finger slipped on her torch, flicking the light on, and the three of them were lit up!

"Intruders!" Jack Frost howled in rage.

He fired an ice-bolt at them, and poor Rachel was frozen solid, her torch in one hand and the party bag in the other.

"Rachel!" cried Kirsty.

But before they could do anything to help her, Kirsty and Elisa were blasted back through the hole in the wall!

Tricksy
Fairies

Kirsty and Elisa were horrified. They
had to rescue Rachel and the tiara – but
how? They pressed themselves against
the outside wall of the tower, listening to
Jack Frost bellowing at the goblins.

"Catch those interfering fairies *now*!"
he howled.

Kirsty and Elisa heard the thunder
of large feet as the goblins hurried
down the tower. They
were shrieking and
grumbling as
they slipped and
scurried down the
steps towards the
battlements.

"What are we
going to do?"
asked Elisa. "We
have to keep the
goblins out of
the way if we're
going to help
Rachel – and get my tiara back."

Suddenly, Kirsty remembered the secret
hiding place in the library.

"I've got an idea, but there's no time to explain," said Kirsty. "We just have to get the goblins to the library."

At that moment, the goblins tumbled out of the tower onto the battlements. As they picked themselves up, Kirsty dived towards them.

"See if you can catch us!" she called to them.

She and Elisa zipped back into the palace, hearing squawks of goblin rage behind them.

They zoomed down the corridor, and
the goblins charged after them, puffing
and panting as they ran.

Elisa led the goblins through side
passageways and unused rooms, carefully
avoiding the places where the other
children might be. Kirsty flew ahead of
her, checking that each room was empty
of children and stewards. At last they
arrived at the library and darted inside,

just before the
goblins caught
up with them.

"Quick,
come and
sit here!"
said Kirsty,
perching on the
revolving bookcase,
next to the vase.

The goblins shut the door and leaned
against it, puffing.

"We've got you now," said the goblin
with the beret. "You can't get away
from us in here, you tricksy fairies!"

"Come and get us, then," said Kirsty,
her hand on the vase.

"What are you going to do?" asked
Elisa.

"When I say 'Go', fly forwards as fast as you can," Kirsty whispered.

The goblins charged towards them and, just at the right moment, Kirsty tipped the vase forwards.

"Go!" she yelled.

As Elisa and Kirsty zoomed across the room, the bookcase whirled around and scooped the goblins into the hiding place behind it!

"It worked!" Kirsty exclaimed. "Now let's rescue Rachel – and your tiara too."

They flew back out of the palace and up to the tower. Carefully, they peered through the broken wall. They could see Rachel frozen in a block of ice on a table. Nearby, Jack Frost was strutting vainly around the tower room in a long yellow robe.

"I'm not sure that yellow suits my skin tone," they heard him muttering. "Perhaps the blue would be better."

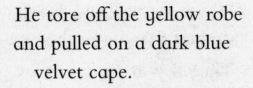

He tore off the yellow robe
and pulled on a dark blue
velvet cape.

"Does this match
the tiara?" he
wondered aloud.
"If only I could see
which robe makes
me look the most
handsome."

"That gives me
an idea," said Kirsty.
"Elisa, can you magic me into a goblin?
If I take Jack Frost a mirror, perhaps that
will distract him so that we can rescue
Rachel and the tiara."

"Oh Kirsty, that sounds like a
wonderful plan," said Elisa with shining
eyes. "But it could be dangerous."

"I don't care," said Kirsty bravely.
"My best friend is in there, and she
needs my help!"

Elisa put her
arms around
Kirsty and
gave her a
warm hug.

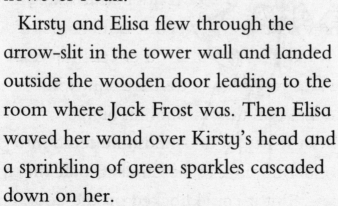

"You're a
very good friend,"
Elisa said. "I'll help
however I can."

Kirsty and Elisa flew through the
arrow-slit in the tower wall and landed
outside the wooden door leading to the
room where Jack Frost was. Then Elisa
waved her wand over Kirsty's head and
a sprinkling of green sparkles cascaded
down on her.

"Skin of green and clumpy feet,
Fool Jack Frost with our deceit."

Kirsty grew back to human size and
felt her nose growing longer and longer.
Her skin took on a greenish tint and
her feet doubled in size. Elisa waved her
wand again, and an ornate
gilt mirror appeared in
Kirsty's hand. She held
it up, and saw
a goblin face staring
back at her.

"Perfect!" she said
with a squawky
goblin giggle.

Elisa fluttered into
her pocket, and Kirsty
knocked on the door.

It flew open at once and Jack Frost stood scowling down at her.

"Well?" he snapped.

Kirsty felt a little bit scared, but then thought of Rachel.

"I've brought you a mirror," she said in a gruff goblin voice.

A vain smile cracked Jack Frost's grumpy frown.

"Excellent!" he declared. "Now I can admire myself properly. Well, don't just stand there! Come in!"

The Spirit of Adventure

Kirsty scurried into the room and went to stand by the candelabra. She held up the mirror so that Jack Frost could see himself.

"Mirror, mirror, in your hand, who's the best in all the land?" he asked.

"Jack Frost, of course," said Kirsty, giving a deep bow.

He smirked and gazed at himself in
the mirror. While he was distracted,
Elisa slipped out of Kirsty's pocket. She
fluttered over to the table and tapped her
wand against the block of ice. Instantly it

melted, and Rachel
was free.

"Thank you,
Elisa!" she
whispered, giving
the little fairy
a hug.

But just then, Jack
Frost spotted Elisa and
Rachel in the mirror's reflection!

"Dratted fairies!" he snarled, lunging
at them.

"Look out!" cried Kirsty.

"Traitor!" Jack Frost shouted.

He raised his wand, but Elisa was
faster. She quickly turned Kirsty back
into a fairy, and
Kirsty zipped
sideways
and
avoided
the
ice-bolt
that
Jack
Frost shot
at her.

Suddenly they
heard a loud thumping
and thundering. The
goblins were racing back up the
tower – they must have escaped from
behind the bookcase!

"Stay still!" roared Jack Frost as Elisa and the girls fluttered around him.

He shot another ice-bolt at them, and then had to clutch at the tiara to stop it falling from his head.

"We just have to get the tiara to slip off his head!" Rachel realised. "Quick – fly around the room as fast as you can!"

The three friends zoomed around the tower room so fast that they looked

blurry to Jack Frost. Ice-bolts hurtled
from his wand as he leapt into the air
to try to catch them. His long fingers
snatched at them, but they stayed just
out of reach.

"Follow me!" cried Rachel.

She led Kirsty and Elisa around the
back of the throne. As the door burst
open and the goblins raced in, the girls
darted out of the hole in the wall and
dropped downwards like stones.

With a yell of rage, Jack Frost lunged
after them, thrusting his head and
shoulders over the broken wall and
peering downwards. He had forgotten
all about the tiara on his head! It
tumbled off and he gave an enraged roar
as Elisa caught it neatly. It shrank to
fairy size at once.

"We've done it!" cheered Rachel and Kirsty together. Jack Frost shook his fist at them as they fluttered down to the battlements. Elisa placed her tiara on her head, and turned to Rachel and Kirsty with sparkling eyes.

"You are very special friends," she said. "I can see that you both carry the spirit of adventure in your hearts. Thank you for everything you have done."

"You're welcome," said Rachel with a big smile.

"It was definitely the most exciting adventure yet!" Kirsty added.

Elisa returned the girls to human-size, and then flicked her wand into the air. A flurry of sparkling jewels flew from the tip and zoomed into the palace through every door and window.

"I have put new jewel stickers all around the palace," said Elisa. "The treasure hunt can go ahead!"

She blew them both tiny fairy kisses and then disappeared in a tiny, glittering whirlwind. Rachel and Kirsty smiled at each other, and then Rachel looked up at the tower.

"I don't think Jack Frost will be causing any more trouble tonight," she said with a laugh. "Come on, let's go and finish the treasure hunt!"

An hour later, all the children were back in the library, and the room was filled with laughter and chatter. Rachel and Kirsty put the final jewel sticker on their crowns and held them up to the light.

"They look lovely!" said a girl called Harriet, holding up her own crown. "What do you think of mine?"

"It's really pretty," said Rachel with a smile.

Victoria and Arthur had been the first to find all their jewel stickers, so they had been declared the winners of the treasure hunt. Their prize was to decide what the next adventure would be.

"Let's play a game," said Arthur, who was wearing his crown. "How about hide and seek?

"Ooh yes, and then let's build dens in the dungeons!" Victoria added.

Kirsty smiled at Rachel as they put their crowns on.

"Now that Elisa has her tiara, everyone's got their spirit of adventure back," she said  with a laugh. "And adventures definitely make life more fun! I wonder what *our* next one will be?"

Now it's time for Kirsty and Rachel to help...

Lizzie the Sweet Treats Fairy

Read on for a sneak peek...

"Having a tea party here in the Orangery is going to be really fun!" Rachel exclaimed to her best friend Kirsty. "I bet that's just what the *real* princes and princesses who lived in Golden Palace used to do."

"I wonder if we're going to have a royal tea of cucumber sandwiches and cream cakes?" Kirsty agreed with a smile. "The Orangery is the perfect place for a special party!"

The Orangery was a gleaming white building with huge arched windows that stood in the grounds of Golden

Palace. Terracotta pots of orange, lemon and lime trees lined the walls of the Orangery, and the air was warm and scented with citrus smells. A spiral staircase in the middle of the building swept up to the wrought-iron balcony overhead, giving spectacular views out of the windows of Golden Palace and its enormous grounds. From the balcony Rachel and Kirsty could see the drawbridge and moat, the lake and ornamental gardens, the maze, the petting zoo and the croquet field.

"Golden Palace looks lovely in the sunshine," Kirsty remarked. The palace had four high towers, one at each corner of the building, and a fifth tower, the highest one, right in the centre. Flags flew on top of all five towers and their golden turrets glittered in the spring sun.

"Aren't we lucky to be here for Kids' Week?" Rachel beamed at Kirsty as they made their way back down the spiral staircase. "Thank you *so* much for inviting me to come." Golden Palace was located in the countryside near Kirsty's home village of Wetherbury, and the girls were spending the spring holiday week there with a group of other children, doing all sorts of fun and interesting activities ...

Read Lizzie the Sweet Treats Fairy to find out what adventures are in store for Kirsty and Rachel!

Meet the fairies, play games
and get sneak peeks at
the latest books!

www.rainbowmagicbooks.co.uk

There's fairy fun for everyone on
our wonderful website.
You'll find great activities, competitions, stories and
fairy profiles, and also a special newsletter.

Get 30% off all Rainbow Magic books at
www.rainbowmagicbooks.co.uk
Enter the code RAINBOW at the checkout.
Offer ends 31 December 2013.

Offer valid in United Kingdom and Republic of Ireland only.

Robyn the Christmas Party Fairy

Rachel and Kirsty are helping to organise a big Christmas party.
But Jack Frost has stolen Robyn the Christmas Party Fairy's
magical objects! The girls must help Robyn,
before the spirit of Christmas is lost forever...

Out now!

Alexandra
the Royal Baby
Fairy

Out in
May 2013

Also available
as an ebook

The whole of Fairyland is very excited - there's going
to be a new royal baby! But when the special baby
goes missing, Rachel and Kirsty are there to help
their friend, Alexandra the Royal Baby Fairy.

www.rainbowmagicbooks.co.uk

Meet the
Princess Fairies

Honor
the Happy Days
Fairy

Demi
the Dressing-Up
Fairy

Anya
the Cuddly Creatures
Fairy

Elisa
the Adventure
Fairy

Lizzie
the Sweet Treats
Fairy

Maddie
the Playtime
Fairy

Eva
the Enchanted Ball
Fairy

**Jack Frost has stolen the Princess Fairies'
tiaras. Kirsty and Rachel must get them back
before all the magic in the world fades away!**

www.rainbowmagicbooks.co.uk